D1824463

Bob Stone has been writing as long as he can remember and has been visiting Formby Pine Woods to see the squirrels as long as he could walk. "A Bushy Tale" is a product of both those loves. This is his first book. You can find him on Facebook at www.facebook.com/bobstone

Holly Bushnell is rapidly becoming sought-after as a designer of murals in schools and homes, as well as greetings cards and prints. "A Bushy Tale" is the first book she has illustrated. You can find her on Facebook at www.facebook.com/hollybushnelldesigns

"A Bushy Tale"

All rights reserved © Bob Stone and Holly Bushnell 2014

No part of this book may be reproduced or transmitted in any form or by any means, graphic, electronic, or mechanical, including photocopying, recording or taping or by any information storage or retrieval system, without the permission in writing from the copywright holders.

The rights of Bob Stone to be identified as the author, and Holly Bushnell as the illustrator of this work have been asserted in accordance with the Copyright, Designs and Patents Act 1988 sections 77 and 78.

IN WHICH SQUISH HAS
A WONDER OR TWO

"Those nuts won't gather themselves, dear."

That's what Squish's mother said more times than Squish could count on his paws.

"Those nuts won't gather themselves."

Squish often wondered about this.

"The nuts fall from the trees by themselves," he thought. "Why can't they gather themselves?"

Squish wondered about a lot of things. His father said that this was the problem with Squish. He spent far too much time wondering about things, and not enough time doing them. But Squish liked to wonder.

He wondered, for example, why Professor Otus, the wise, old, long-eared owl who ran the school said it was good to read books. Every time Squish tried to read one and was just getting to a good bit, his mother told him he should be outside on such a nice day, playing, or gathering nuts with the other young squirrels. After all, those nuts won't ... but then, you know what nuts won't do themselves, don't you?

Squish wondered why the other animals did not worry about collecting food and storing it up.

"Maybe," he thought, "they always have plenty of food and don't need to store any."

He kept meaning to ask some of his friends, but somehow never got round to it.

Squish wondered if Whitetip, who lived in the next tree might like to help him with his gathering one day.

She had a bright white tip to her tail, which no other squirrel had, which was where she got her name.

"I wonder why I can't just ask her," he thought. "Every time I go to ask I just end up talking too much about everything else."

On one particular summer's day, when the sun was shining through the branches of the big trees in The Woods and making the ground look like it had patches of gold growing on it, Squish was sitting in the drey and wondering again about gathering nuts. He knew squirrels gathered nuts to eat and to hide them for all the times when there were no nuts growing on the trees. He knew that the best gatherers had lots of really good hiding places where they could keep nuts safe. He just thought there must be a better way of doing it. Even the quickest collector could only carry one nut in his paws and maybe two in his mouth (if he had a really big mouth, like Scritch, Squish's big brother). Squish wondered if there was a way of gathering lots of nuts at the same time, so there would be more time to do other things, like reading or playing in the trees. He thought that one day he might come up with a better way. One day, but probably not today.

Squish knew better than to ask his mother and father about things. His mother was usually very busy and told him to ask his father. His father usually explained in a way which went on so long that Squish ended up more confused than ever. Squish remembered once, when he was quite young, asking his father where his name came from. He knew that, unlike lots of animals, squirrels are not given their name at birth, but a bit later when their parents get to know them and so know what name suits.

"Well," Squish's father began, "you were named after your grandfather."

"Was he called Squish too?" Squish asked, thinking this might be a short explanation for once.

"No, he was called Forestson The Most Magnificent Bushytail The Third," his father replied.

"Why The Third?" Squish wanted to know.

"Because his father was The Second. And *his* father was Forestson The Most Magnificent Bushytail. The First one. You know how all my friends call me Magnus? It's short for Forestson the Most Magnificent Bushytail the Fourth."

"But I should be called The Most Mag ... Magnicifent Bushytail the one ... two ... three ... four ... oh, but there's Scamp and Scritch too. I've lost count now." Squish frowned. Magnus laughed.

"Yes, but your grandfather ended up being known as Squish after he went up the Biggest Tree. You know about the Biggest Tree, don't you?"

"It's the one old squirrels go up and don't come back down."

"Not just old squirrels. Your grandfather went up the Biggest Tree when he wasn't so old because he was a dreamer."

"But why?" Squish asked. Why? was something Squish often asked.

"Because he was dreaming instead of looking where he was going when he crossed the big black path made by the Giant Nofurs. That's how he ended up being called Forestson Squishtail the First. You are Forestson Squishtail the Second because you have always been a dreamer since you were tiny. We just call you Squish because it's quicker. And that young Squish, is why it's not good to spend so much time dreaming."

Squish was left none the wiser, and carried on dreaming, or wondering about things, as he called it. But he never tried to cross the big black path. Not until the Squish and the other Reds heard that the Greys were coming.

IN WHICH WE LEARN ABOUT THE GIANT
NOFURS AND THE BIG BLACK PATH

The big black path hadn't always been there. No squirrels could remember a time before the path came, but the old squirrels told stories which they had been told by their parents and grandparents about the days before the path. No-one could say how long ago it was, but there was a time when the Woods were all there was, stretching to the end of the world and back. It was a happier, safer time; a time before the Giant Nofurs started putting big black paths everywhere. All young squirrels were told by their parents to stay away from the big black path and never ever try to cross it. Any animal that tried to cross the path went straight up the Biggest Tree.

The Giant Nofurs used the big black path to move about very quickly in huge boxes which were made of something Squish's father called "met-all". Squish assumed this was why they moved so fast; because they had so many other Nofurs to meet. One of these boxes had certainly met Squish's grandfather with very unpleasant results. This was why Squish and his brothers and sisters were always taught to stay away from the big black path; because when the

Nofurs were sitting in their met-all boxes they could not see small animals like squirrels and hedgehogs, not even at night when the boxes had big, frightening lights on. And the Nofurs really enjoyed riding as quickly as they could in their boxes, which was something the animals found hard to understand. Most animals like to take life at more of a steady pace, unless they are in danger, when they can run quickly enough by themselves, thank you very much.

Squish found the Giant Nofurs a funny kind of animal for lots of reasons, not just their big met-all boxes. He didn't understand why an animal would choose to take most of its fur off, and then, when it was cold, put coloured coverings on to keep warm.

"Why don't they just keep their fur on?" Squish asked his friend Brian, a young badger. (Brian's badger name was something like Snuffledigsnort, but other animals found badger hard to speak so they all called him Brian).

"My Dad says it's because some of them can't grow much fur, so they all take it off. I don't know why some of them can't grow it. Maybe there's something wrong with them."

"It must feel funny having no fur. They don't seem to climb trees much either," Squish said.

"They don't dig setts or collect twigs," Brian pointed out. "They're not much use at all, in fact. I wonder what they're for."

"They bring nuts and throw them to us," Squish said.

"Which you take away and hide, thank you very much," said Brian.

"You don't like nuts," Squish told him.

"I know. You'd think the Nofurs would bring something for us as well. Like worms."

"I think they only come to see squirrels. That's why they bring nuts."

"You would think that," Brian said, "with your red fur and your bushy tail. Not everyone likes red, you know. Some people like black and white and grey, too."

Squish knew that badgers could be quite touchy about only being black, white and grey, when other animals like squirrels and foxes had lovely red fur, and some of the birds like the bluetits and the goldfinches had bright yellow and blue feathers. Even the starlings (who Squish was a bit frightened of because they were so noisy) had lots of colours. Brian also didn't like talking about fur because his was a bit curlier than most badgers, but no-one really mentioned it. It was one of those things that the other animals didn't talk about with their voices but talked about with their eyes instead. Anyway, Squish thought, Brian may grow out of it.

There were some Nofurs, who were all green, like the grass or the spring leaves. Squish's father said they were called Rainjars or something. Squish did not understand what they had to do with rain, because you didn't see them much when it was raining. But Squish was told that they were good Nofurs, who came and made dreys in the trees for squirrels who didn't want to make them for themselves.

The other Giant Nofurs who weren't Rainjars did other funny things, which Squish didn't understand. One day, he was gathering nuts and acorns with his brother Forestson Scamper the Best Champion Acorn Collector, or Scamp as everyone called him. Scamp liked to play tricks on the Nofurs. His favourite one was to sit on a branch, drop acorn shells onto any Nofurs standing below and run away. He watched from another branch as the Nofurs brushed themselves as if they didn't know what had landed on them. Their faces wrinkled up and they made funny eww noises. Squish wasn't sure why they did this, or why some of the other squirrels called Scamp 'Squit' but they all seemed to think it was very funny.

On this particular day, a group of Nofurs had stopped near the trees where Squish and Scamp were working.

"Look," said Squish. "Why are they doing that?"

The Nofurs kept taking little boxes out and pointing them at each other or at the squirrels and sometimes there was a bright flash like when the sun suddenly appears through the trees. The Nofurs seemed to enjoy this like nothing else.

"I don't know," Scamp replied. "They seem to do it more and more. Scritch says that if you let them point their box at you they give you more nuts. Watch."

Scamp hopped nearer the Nofurs.

"Be careful!" Squish called, but Scamp wasn't listening. He stopped as near to the Nofurs as he dared and sat looking at them. The Nofurs were delighted with this and all pointed their little boxes at Scamp. Then some of them threw so many nuts to Scamp that he could not carry them and Squish had to come and help. This prompted more pointing and more nuts came flying over.

These Nofurs aren't so bad, Squish thought. They

might build big dangerous black paths, but they seem to love us squirrels and always bring lots of nuts.

Squish didn't know then just how dangerous the big black path could be until the day the squirrels heard the Greys were coming and Squish had to cross it.

THREE

IN WHICH WE FIND OUT
MORE ABOUT THE GREYS

No-one really knew where the Greys came from. There was a time, a long time ago, when the Reds were the only kind of squirrel. They lived happily, gathering nuts and acorns. No-one really bothered them and they bothered nobody. But Squish remembered one day when his father sat him down, just as he had done with Squish's older brothers and sisters.

"Squish," he said, in the voice he used when he wanted to say Something Serious. "You must watch out for the Greys."

"What's the Graze?" Squish had asked. He had only heard the word "graze" used about animals which eat grass, like deer. He hoped his father was not warning him about animals like that, because he quite liked deer. They seemed very gentle animals who just liked wandering about nibbling plants.

"The Greys are other squirrels. They don't have red fur like us. Sometimes they have bits of red on them but they are mostly grey."

"Is it like how Whitetip has a bit of white on her tail?" Squish asked.

"Not really," Magnus answered. "Whitetip is a Red with a tiny bit of white. They Greys are just grey."

"With bits of red."

"Yes, Squish, with bits of red.

"Why do I need to watch out for them?"

"Well, young Squish," his father said, "they say that the Greys are not very nice squirrels."

"What, like Scamp when he's in a bad mood?" Squish remembered a time when Scritch had put some spiky horse chestnut shells in Scamp's bed and Scamp had been in a very bad mood.

"No, Squish, worse than that. Everyone has bad moods sometimes, but are happy the rest of the time. From what I have heard, the Greys are in a bad mood all the time."

"Why? What are they cross about?"

"No-one knows. They just are."

"Maybe they don't like being grey when we are lovely and red," Squish suggested.

"I don't know," Magnus replied with his Thinking Face on. "Look at the finches. The Greens and the Golds and the Chaffinches all have different colour feathers but they seem to get on. There are different families of deer and owls and sparrows, but they live side by side. I don't think the Greys are like that because of the colour of their fur. I have heard it is because the Greys are selfish."

Squish knew all about selfish. He had been taught not to be selfish from when he was a very small squirrel. His parents had always taught their children that it didn't matter how big and tasty the nuts and acorns were that they found, they should always share them and not keep all the best ones for themselves. After all, they were told, one day you might not be able to find many nice ones, and you will be glad if others shared with you.

"Why are they selfish?" Squish asked. "Don't they want to share?"

"They don't want to share with us," his father explained. "I believe that there are lots more Greys than there are Reds and so the Greys want all the nuts and acorns for themselves."

"But that's silly," Squish said. "There's usually lots of nuts and acorns. There is always enough to go round everybody!"

"The Greys don't care. They are not bothered if there are more nuts than they need. They just want to have them all. They don't want anyone else to have them. But there is another reason you must watch out for the Greys."

Squish was getting quite scared now. Selfish squirrels who were always in a bad mood and wanted all the nuts and acorns were bad enough. What else could there be?

"Greys carry an illness," Magnus told him. "You know how you got the sniffles that time and had to stay in bed? It's like that but much much worse. I've heard other Reds say that this illness does not affect the Greys, but if we Reds catch it, we go straight up the Biggest Tree. That is why, young Squish, if you see a Grey, you must stay away from it and you must come and tell me. Do you understand?"

Squish understood. He was very young when his father told him this, and did not want to go up the Biggest Tree yet. He and his brother and sisters often played a game called What Would You Do If You See A Grey? This usually involved running away or up a tree as quickly as you could. Their parents watched them play this game and were glad they played it. Squish heard his parents talking about it one day.

"Do you think the Greys will come to the Woods?" his mother asked in a little voice Squish had not heard before. Squish's mother was usually the one who did the telling-off if the young squirrels were naughty and never sounded scared of anything.

"I don't know," Magnus replied, holding his wife's paw tightly. "I have heard that they are getting closer. I'm glad we have taught the children what to do."

Squish thought about this sometimes, when he was out on his own. They are getting closer. Sometimes, if he heard a rustling in the bushes his heart started to beat faster and he worried it might be a Grey, but it was usually a hedgehog coming out blinking from its Deep Sleep, or a young fox looking for something good to eat. But he thought about his mother's little voice and how serious his father had sounded and always tried to be careful.

But if the Greys were getting closer, they had not come to the Woods yet. The day the squirrels heard the Greys were coming, is when our story really begins. If I were you, I would ask for the light to be left on for a while, because parts of the story might be a bit scary.

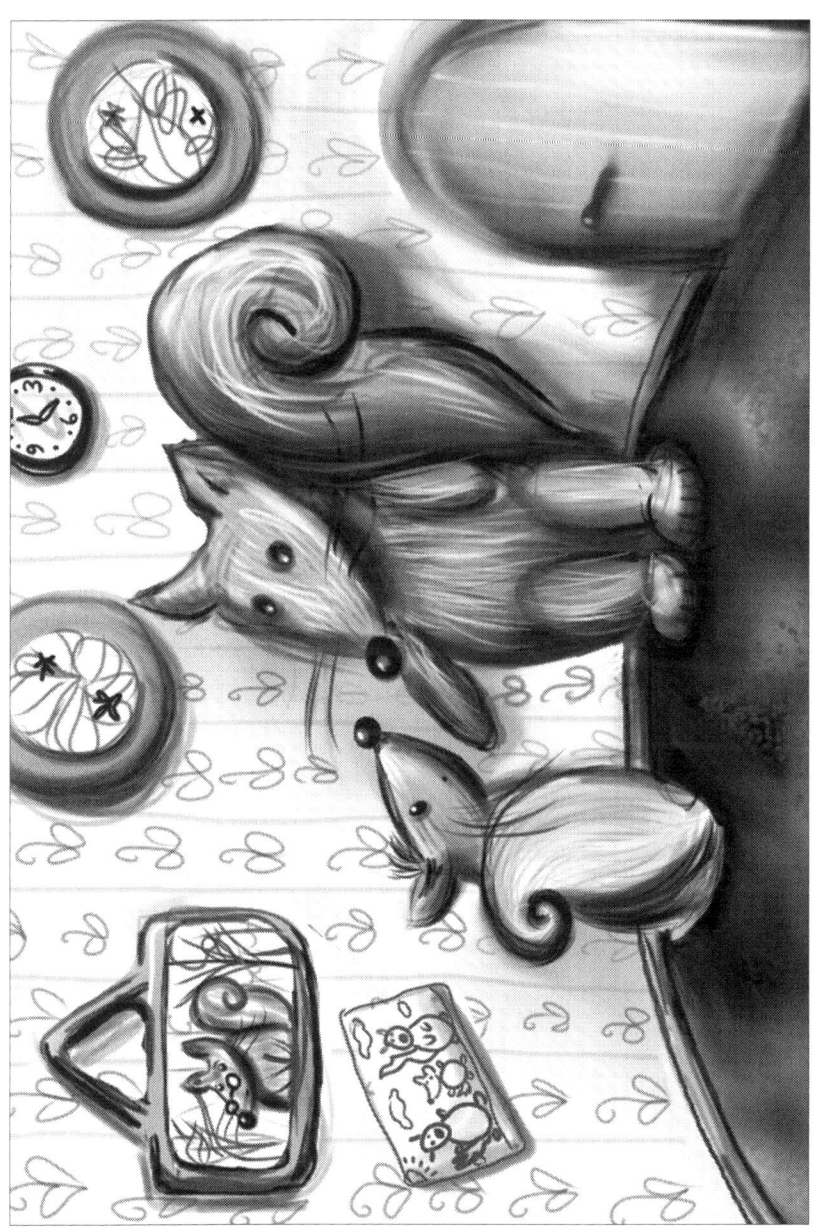

FOUR

IN WHICH EVERYONE THINKS
THE GREYS HAVE ARRIVED

No-one could really agree on who saw the first Grey. Professor Otus, who taught the young animals to read and who should have been reliable said he saw a Grey near the Woods one night while he was out flying. He said he saw the Grey sitting looking towards the Woods.

"It looked like it was waiting for something," Professor Otus said. "I don't know what it was waiting for."

Two bluetits tweeted that they had seen a Grey sitting in the shadow of a large old pine tree.

"We don't know what it was doing," they tweeted. "It was just sitting there. It might have been an old root that looked like a Grey."

A young fox friend of Squish's, whose name in fox was Grrwoffwoof, but who was known as Colin to everyone who didn't speak fox, said he saw the Grey earlier the same evening.

"I saw it running towards the Pine Woods," Colin said. "I don't know why it was running."

Several small hedgehogs (whose names need not bother us right now because they were clearly making their story up to impress everyone) swore that they had chased away three enormous Greys.

"They had big sticks and everything," the hedgehogs said. "But when they saw us they ran away."

Whitetip knocked on Squish's drey to say that some of her friends were saying that the Greys were already in the Woods, but were hiding. Squish really wanted to say to her, "Don't worry, Whitetip. You'll be safe with me," but somehow it came out as "I don't think they are." It was obvious that Whitetip was frightened by the thought of the Greys and so were most of the other squirrels. It was clear that if the Greys were very near then something had to be done.

One evening, Squish's father and some of the other older squirrels met to talk about what to do. They met in the drey Squish shared with his parents and his brothers and sisters, but all the young squirrels were sent to a drey in the next tree for the night. Squish tried to argue.

"We want to do something!" he said.

"I'm sorry, Squish," Magnus said. "I know you all want to help, but there are things which do not concern young squirrels."

Squish could see that his father was very serious so he went with his brothers and sisters to the next tree. Squish was tempted to stay inside the drey, because this was the drey where Whitetip lived. But much as he would usually have liked Whitetip's company, this time Squish wanted to be on his own. He was also very curious about what the older squirrels were discussing. So while Scamp, Scritch and their sisters played inside the drey with the other young squirrels, Squish sat outside on a branch and tried to listen to snatches of the older squirrels' conversation as they drifted over on the evening breeze.

"... protect the acorns ..." he heard, and "... mustn't lose the trees..." but the older squirrels were talking in low voices so it was hard to hear. The other young squirrels werc also making a lot of noise as they played inside the drey.

After a while, Scamp came out and sat with him. Scamp was laughing and had clearly been enjoying himself.

"You should have - ha ha - seen it, Squish!" he said, stopping every few words to laugh again. "We told Whitetip that the Greys would cut off the white tip of her tail and she started crying! She's such a baby!"

Squish was suddenly angry. It was bad enough that the Greys had made everything so serious, but he hated the idea of his brothers upsetting Whitetip.

"You leave Whitetip alone!" he snapped. "You shouldn't tease her like that."

Squish did not argue with his brother very often and this made Scamp suddenly stop laughing.

"Don't worry, Squish," Scamp said. "I know you're scared but Dad and the other older squirrels won't let the Greys hurt you. Anyway, Scritch and I will fight them off!"

Squish did not feel like replying. The way he felt at that moment, he didn't think he needed anyone to fight for him. Scamp went back inside, muttering something about "sulking squirrels".

Squish sat for a while trying to calm down. Everything was suddenly getting very serious and he felt like the world he had always known had been taken away and replaced with a scarier world he didn't like. He was so lost in thought that he did not realise he was no longer alone.

"Scamp said you stuck up for me," Whitetip said. "Thank you."

"That's okay," Squish replied. Now Whitetip was sitting next to him he couldn't think of anything else to say.

"Your brother's an idiot," Whitetip said. "He just makes jokes all the time. He isn't clever like you."

"I'm not clever," Squish said. "I'm a dreamer. That's what my Dad says."

"Well I think that's the same thing. You think about things," Whitetip said. "I think you should be over there with the older squirrels."

"The older squirrels will sort it out," Squish said. "They will know what to do."

"I still think you should be there. It's like nobody cares how we feel," Whitetip said. Squish thought for a moment.

"It's not that they don't care," he said. "They are all worried about something and they won't tell us what it is. My Dad says there are things we young squirrels don't need to know."

"Well I think we should know. I'm scared of the Greys, Squish. We all are. Can you find out what they are saying?"

Whitetip touched Squish's paw with her own for a second. For that second Squish felt like he could fight all the Greys by himself.

Before he even knew he was doing it, Squish had jumped from one tree to the next. It was a very big jump for a small squirrel, but Squish balanced himself with his tail as he had been taught, and leaped into the air. Whenever he made a big jump like this, he always thought that this must be how the birds feel when they fly and how wonderful it must be to soar away into the sky. Squirrels don't have wings and so have to make do with jumping, but knowing Whitetip was watching made Squish feel like he was flying too. He landed neatly on a branch and sat outside his family's drey listening very quietly. This is what he heard:

"... we don't even know what the Greys want, Magnus," one older squirrel was saying. "They might want to be friends. We should talk to them."

"I'm sorry Russetcoat," Squish's father said, "but if you think that, you are a fool. You know we can't let the Greys near us. Imagine if the illness they carry starts to spread. Anyway, we do know what the

Greys want. They want our nuts and our acorns. All of them. And you know what that means."

"But what about the ones we have hidden?" another squirrel asked.

"They are squirrels too," Squish's father replied. "They know all about hiding nuts. I know the other animals laugh at us and say we have forgotten where we put them..."

"Sssh!" Russetcoat said. "Someone might hear."

"There's nobody here but squirrels, Russ. But you are right. We don't want the other animals to know the Squirrels' Secret."

This was enough for Squish. The squirrels had a secret! He waited to hear if his father would say what the secret was, but he started talking about acorns, using big words Squish had never heard before. As quietly as he could, Squish made the leap back to the other tree. Whitetip was waiting for him.

"What are they saying?" Whitetip asked.

"I couldn't hear," Squish said. Even though he wanted to tell Whitetip what he had heard, he needed time to think about it. He also quite liked the idea of having a secret of his own.

Squish and the other young squirrels spent the night at the next door tree. The older squirrels carried on talking until long after the young squirrels' bedtime. But Squish found it hard to sleep, even though the drey was comfortable and warm and he was very tired. What was the Squirrels' Secret? And what did it have to do with acorns and the Greys? He decided that as soon as he could, he would find out.

FIVE

IN WHICH SQUISH LEARNS
THE SQUIRRELS' SECRET

The next morning, Squish woke up early. It was so early that there was still mist around the higher branches of the trees and the branches were damp and slippery. Squish waiting patiently until his mother came to collect the young squirrels and bring them back to their drey for breakfast.

Squish did not really enjoy his breakfast, even though it was acorn mash, which was one of his favourites. He was too busy thinking about the Squirrels' Secret. He knew that he would not just be able to find out about it by accident. That was how secrets stayed secret. He would have to be very brave and ask his father, and the thought of this made him quite scared. His father was still being very serious, even though he pretended to enjoy Scamp's jokes at the breakfast table.

After breakfast, Squish's father went to sit on a pile of pine needles and leaves, which was where he sat when he wanted to do some thinking. This usually meant that nobody should disturb him, but Squish knew that he had to. The thought of the Squirrels'

Secret was too big in his head to keep there without saying something. He crept over to his father and sat next to him.

"Yes, young Squish?" his father said. "Do you want to say something, or did you just feel like keeping an old squirrel company?"

"What's the Squirrels' Secret?" Squish blurted out. He could not help himself.

Magnus turned and looked at him. His face was very stern and Squish felt like running away.

"Where did you hear about that?" he asked.

"I-I don't know," Squish stammered. "I-I just heard someone saying."

Magnus's face stayed very stern for a moment, but then he surprised Squish by smiling.

"Squish, do you really think I don't know the smell of my own children? Even through the walls of a drey?"

"I'm sorry," Squish said, hanging his head. "I'm sorry I spied on you. But it was all so serious and scary and I wanted to know what was happening."

"You have always been inquisitive," his father said,

with another smile. "You have always asked more questions than any of your brothers and sisters."

"I like to know things," Squish told him.

"It is good to know things," Magnus said. "Come with me."

At first, Squish did not know whether to follow his father. He thought he might be about to be punished for being inky-whatever-it-was-he-had-said. But his father had said it was good to know things, hadn't he? So Squish followed his father out of the drey and down the trunk of the tree. They stopped at the bottom. Squish's father sat and looked up at the tree. It was so tall that Squish could not see the top.

"What is that?" Magnus asked, pointing a paw at the tree.

"It's ... it's a tree?" said Squish, who thought it might be a trick question.

"Yes it is. It is a very tall, very old tree. Do you know where it came from?"

"It didn't come from anywhere!" Squish exclaimed. "It's always been there. It's where we live."

"Oh Squish," his father said, shaking his head. "You are very young."

Squish's father dug amongst the oak leaves on the ground and pulled out an acorn.

"What is this?" he asked.

"It's an acorn," Squish told him. "Everyone knows that."

"And where does it come from?"

"Acorns come from the oak trees," Squish answered, reciting it like he had learned at Professor Otus's school.

"That's right. And oak trees come from acorns."

This was such a silly idea that Squish laughed.

"How can something that big," he pointed to the tree, "come from something that small?" He pointed to the acorn in his father's paws.

"That," said his father, "is the Squirrel's secret. Our tree has not always been there. It has been there a very long time, longer than any of us can remember. My father lived here before us, and his father lived there before that. But once, a very very long time before our family lived in this tree, it was just an acorn."

"But a tree is a tree and an acorn is, well, it's an acorn!" Squish was very confused.

"What do we do with acorns?" his father asked.

"We eat them!" Squish knew the answer to this one. "Mum makes mash and ..."

"What else do we do with them?"

Squish thought about this. He knew the answer

"We hide them?" he asked.

"Yes, Squish we hide them. Why do we hide them?"

"Professor Otus said it was so other animals don't eat them and we have plenty of food when the acorns and nuts don't fall."

"That is true. But not all animals eat acorns and nuts. Brian and the other badgers don't eat acorns, do they?"

"No," said Squish wrinkling his snout. "They eat worms. It's disgusting."

"There is another reason why we hide nuts and acorns and pine cones. That is the Squirrels' Secret too. Come with me."

Magnus led him a short way across the floor of the Pine Woods. He pointed his paw at a small plant which was growing out of the fallen pine needles and leaves.

"Do you know what this is?" his father asked.

Squish thought about his Plant Lessons with Professor Otus, but he hadn't really been listening that day.

"I'll tell you," his father said. "That is a very young oak tree. If it is left alone, one day it will be as big as our oak tree and other squirrels will be able to live in it. Everything is small when it starts. You were very small once. So was I. So was everything. Now look at this."

Squish's father carefully dug the soil away from the bottom of the plant and Squish could just about make out what looked like a broken acorn. Squish looked closer, and to his surprise, the stem of the plant seemed to be growing out of the acorn.

"And that is the biggest secret of all," his father said, pushing the soil back around the bottom of the plant. "Oak trees grow from acorns. Acorns grow on oak trees. If we do not have trees, we have no food. We would have no twigs and leaves to build our dreys. The birds would have nowhere to make nests, or branches to sing on. Nobody would have anywhere to live or food to eat. Now do you understand? That is why squirrels hide nuts and acorns. It is because we know that if we do, new trees will come. That way your children will have trees to live in, and so will their children after them."

"But why is it a secret?" Squish asked. He thought he was beginning to understand some of what his father was saying. "All the other animals think we hide the nuts and forget about them. They laugh at us."

"I know," his father said. "We let them think that. They are all too busy with their lives to think about the future. They do not know that we are laughing at them. And that, young Squish, is the Squirrels' secret. You mustn't tell anyone."

"I won't," Squish said. He was not sure if he understood it enough to tell anyone.

Later, when the mist had cleared, Squish and his brothers and sisters went out to gather nuts and acorns. Now, as well as watching out for Greys, Squish had to think about where he was hiding the nuts and acorns he had gathered. He had so much on his mind that he forgot his promise to his father. When Squish had to cross the big black path, he ended up telling everyone the Squirrels' Secret.

IN WHICH A SMALL IDEA
GROWS INTO A BIG PLAN

Squish thought a great deal about what his father had told him over the next few days. Every time he passed an oak tree he thought about how it had once been an acorn. Every time he hid nuts and acorns away, he thought carefully about where he was hiding them. He always tried to make sure they were hidden in a good place to grow, where the soil was soft and dark and damp. He just thought it was a pity that one day soon, the Greys were going to come and take all the nuts and acorns for themselves. He wished he could come up with a way of stopping this from happening.

He was talking about it one day with Colin and Brian. He had to talk to someone about it, but couldn't talk to his father because he could see his father was already worried about it. He couldn't talk to Scritch or Scamp because they would just make a joke out of it. He would have liked to talk to Whitetip, but her father was keeping her and her brothers and sisters indoors most of the time. Who better to talk to, then, than his friends? The only trouble was, he had to do it without telling them the Squirrels' Secret.

Squish and his friends had wandered through the Pine Woods and were getting near the big black path. They were not supposed to go that far on their own, but they liked to watch the Nofurs whizzing past in their met-all boxes.

"They don't seem to care about anything," Squish said, as one of the boxes went past so close to them that a rush of wind shook the trees and ruffled their fur. "I bet they don't have to worry about things like the Greys coming to steal their food."

"What are you squirrels going to do about it?" Colin asked.

"I don't know," Squish told him. "The older squirrels are talking about it a lot."

"Mmmffing mmff," said Brian, whose snout was in a pile of leaves. Brian's snout was often digging about in a pile of something. He realised no-one had heard him and looked up, soil still clinging to his snout. "They're not doing anything then. Just talking."

"I don't think talking will stop the Greys," Squish said. "We need a plan. But no-one will listen to me. I'm too young."

"How about hiding the nuts?" Colin suggested.

"They thought of that, but the Greys are squirrels too and they know all about where we would hide them."

"I don't see how," Brian said, laughing. "Even you Reds don't know where you hide them. Everyone knows the squirrels keep forgetting where they've hidden stuff."

"That's not true!" Squish shouted, suddenly angry. Colin and Brian were shocked. They had never seen Squish angry before. Squish was a bit shocked by himself too. "We do know where we hide things. We just don't tell anyone."

They sat on a clump of grass near the big black path and thought.

"If it was another bunch of foxes trying to steal our food, we'd fight them," Colin said.

Foxes often had fights. Colin's older brother was nicknamed "Halfear" because he had a small piece of the tip of his left ear missing. He said it had happened when he fought off two other foxes, but everyone knew he had really caught it on a bramble. All the same, all the other animals were a bit afraid of the foxes. Squish was not afraid of Colin though. He had never been in a fight and preferred to read or wander about in the Woods with his friends.

"We can't fight the Greys," Squish said. "There are too many of them to fight."

"You want to do what we do," Brian said. "Dig tunnels underground and live there. The Greys wouldn't find you underground."

Badgers liked it underground. They liked being in the dark with lots of worms to eat. Animals which lived underground, like badgers and rabbits were always surprising the other animals by suddenly appearing out of holes in the ground.

"Squirrels can't live underground," Squish said. "We don't really like the dark. We like to sit in the trees where we can see everything."

"So you can't hide the nuts, you can't fight and you won't live underground," Colin said. "So what are you going to do?"

"It sounds to me," said Brian, "like you're just going to give up. You're just going to hand the nuts and acorns over to the Greys."

Squish thought hard. Now they had talked about it, it did sound like that.

"Anyway," Colin said, "I don't see what the problem is. There are always nuts and acorns around. It's not like you have to hunt for your food."

Squish didn't like to think about that. He knew that foxes learn to hunt when they are very young. That was another reason why the other animals were afraid of the foxes. He also knew Colin was wrong. If the Greys took all the nuts and acorns, there might not be any more. He was very close to telling his friends the Squirrels' Secret, but he stopped himself.

"I've got to come up with a plan," Squish said. "If nobody else will do it, then I will."

That night, when Squish was tucked up in the drey and his mother and father thought he was asleep, he thought about everything Colin and Brian had said. All the other animals had different ideas about what they would do, but none of the ideas were what squirrels would do. Then it suddenly struck him. What if ...? But no, he shook his head. That couldn't possibly work. Could it? But the idea wouldn't go away. Squish finally went to sleep with thoughts whirling around in his head.

He woke up early the next morning and the thoughts were still there. Often, if you have thoughts late at night when you are trying to get to sleep, they disappear into dreams and are gone by the morning. The fact that Squish's thoughts were still there, meant that they were real. He had An Idea.

He got up straight away. His mother and father were already up.

"You're up very early, young Squish," his father said. "Couldn't you sleep?"

"Not really," Squish told him. "I think I know how to stop the Greys."

His father laughed.

"Really?" he asked. "And how is a young squirrel like you planning to stop the Greys, when all the older squirrels can't come up with an idea between them?"

"That's because you're looking at it the wrong way," Squish said. "I want to call a meeting."

As soon as he had said it, Squish realised that his father was not laughing any more.

SEVEN

IN WHICH A SMALL SQUIRREL
TRIES TO CALL A BIG MEETING

"You can't call a meeting," Squish's father said. He did not seem sure whether or not he wanted to laugh again.

"Why not?" Squish asked. He really didn't think his father was taking him seriously.

"No-one has called a meeting for years and years. The last time was when Professor Otus wanted to set up lessons to teach young animals to read. But that was Professor Otus, not you."

"Why not me?" Squish wanted to know.

"You're a very young squirrel, not a wise old owl. Young squirrels don't call meetings. Now come and have your breakfast."

Squish realised that he was quite hungry, so he sat down while his mother served the acorn mash.

"Squish wants to call a meeting," his father said.

"That's nice," his mother replied. Squish thought

she was too busy making the breakfast to listen.

"I still don't see why I can't," Squish said.

Magnus stopped eating.

"Older animals can call meetings for very important things. But meetings are very rare. I can only remember the one Professor Otus called and I don't know when there was one before that. Not in my time. Meetings are for all the animals, so it has to be about something very important which will affect everyone. No-one will come to a meeting which is just about squirrels. Who will be interested in that?"

"But it does affect everyone. Everyone needs the trees. If the Greys take all the nuts and acorns, there won't be any trees for anyone!"

Squish's father smiled. Squish thought it looked like a sad smile.

"You mean well, young Squish," he said. "I'll tell you what, you go ahead and call your meeting. We'll see what happens."

"I will," Squish replied, finishing the last of his acorn mash.

As he left the drey, he thought he heard his father say "It will never work." We will see what happens, Squish thought, as he raced down the trunk of the tree. We will.

The first person Squish went to see was Professor Otus. He knew that Professor Otus very supposed to be the oldest owl in the Woods and always seemed quite stern, especially with young animals who did not pay attention in his lessons. But Squish also knew that the Professor talked to all the other birds. There was no use in Squish talking to the birds, because all they seemed to want to do was fly around twittering and tweeting to each other. If anyone could get the birds to come to a meeting, it would be Professor Otus.

Professor Otus lived in a nest in the branches of a very old tree. There was a battered old wooden sign on the trunk of the tree which read "Professor Wikiwoo Otus, M.I.W.O. (Member of the Institute of Wisest Owls)." Squish had been to the nest many times for lessons and he knew that it was full of books and not much else. Animals' books, by the way, are not like the books you know. They are written on leaves and pieces of bark in writing you won't be able to read. You have probably seen some animals' books lying around and not realised what they were.

Squish was nervous about going to the Professor's nest, because it usually meant having lessons and being told off. He knocked on the nest and waited.

"Hoo-who's there?" Professor Otus called from inside.

"It's Squish, Professor Otus, sir," Squish said.

"Come in, young Squish," called Professor Otus. "It's not time for lessons yet, is it?"

"No sir," Squish said, as he went into the nest. He could hardly see the Professor behind piles of books. All he could see was a pair of bright yellow eyes looking out at him.

"Professor Otus, sir, I want to call a meeting. Would you please tell the birds? It will be at sundown today in the clearing in the middle of the woods."

"A meeting?" Professor Otus asked. "And why would a young squirrel like you-hooo call a meeting?"

"We have to stop the Greys from taking the nuts and acorns. I want everyone to help."

"Ah," said the Professor. "The Grey Squirrels. Well,

young Squish, I'd love to help, but you see I have all these books to read. I have to teach all you young animals, so I'm very busy."

"But if the Greys take the acorns there won't be any more trees," Squish said. "Where will the books come from then? Where will the birds make their nests?"

"Now, Squish," Professor Otus said. "There will always be trees. I'm very old and there have always been trees as long as I have lived here."

"Well if you're too busy, will you please tell the birds?"

"I'll see if I have time," Professor Otus said and went back to his reading. Squish thanked him and left.

Squish decided to go and see the badgers next. Brian's father was always very friendly, and Squish wanted to talk to a friendly animal after seeing Professor Otus. He found the entrance to the badgers' sett and knocked on a root near the opening. Brian's father came to the entrance. He seemed to be covered in soil, but this was nothing new to Squish. Brian's father was always covered in soil. That is why everyone called him Earthface, but in badger that was a very great compliment, because it meant you were the best digger.

"Hello, Squish," he said, shaking himself. "You're up very early. I think Brian's still in bed."

"I wanted to see you," Squish explained. "I'm calling a meeting and I'd like you to tell the other badgers, please."

"A meeting? Is this about the Grey Squirrels?"

"Yes it is," Squish said. "I have a plan to stop them and I need everyone's help."

"Well that's very clever of you," Earthface said. "But we're a bit busy at the moment. Tunnels to dig and all that. There are some big tree roots we need to dig round."

"But if they Greys take the acorns, there won't be any trees!" Squish said. "You won't have any roots to dig around."

"There will always be trees," Earthface said. "Everyone knows that."

Squish told him when and where the meeting would be, thanked him and left.

Next, Squish went to see the foxes. He usually tried not to speak to Colin's father. His name was Ray, which was short for Rabbitscourge Raynard the Swiftest Hunter of All Time. The foxes called him something else in their own language, but it just sounded like a lot of snarls and growls. Fox was a very strange language, Squish thought.

Squish was nearly at the foxes' home, when there was a rustle in the undergrowth, and a red snout filled with teeth popped out. It was followed by the rest of Ray.

"Hello Squish," Ray said, with a grin which Squish thought at first meant he was about to be breakfast. "Sorry. Something in my teeth. What can I do for you? Are looking for Colin?"

"No, sir," Squish said. "I wanted to see you. I'm calling a meeting about the Greys."

"A meeting, eh?" Ray asked in a voice most people would use when they say "a barbeque" and licked his lips. "Well I'm not sure what your Greys have to do with us foxes."

"They're going to take all the nuts and acorns," Squish told him.

"Can't be doing with nuts and acorns," Ray replied. "Too dry if you know what I mean. Anyway, we're very busy. We have a big hunt planned."

"But without the nuts and acorns, there won't be any trees. Without the trees there won't be any of the - er - things you like to hunt."

"Don't be silly, Squish," Ray said. "There will always be trees. And there will always be things to hunt."

Squish told him where the meeting was to be held, thanked him and left very quickly.

For the rest of the morning, Squish went round talking to the other animals, but the answer was always the same. They were too busy. The hedgehogs were busy making their nests for The Big Sleep and didn't seem to understand that without trees they would have nothing to make their nests out of. The rabbits were very busy doing something and anyway, for some reason they didn't really want to come to a meeting if the foxes were going to be there. Even the smallest mice and voles said they had something more important to do, even though everyone knew mice didn't do anything important. Nobody seemed interested in the meeting. Squish went back to his drey feeling very small and sad.

"How did it go?" his father asked.

"Nobody cares about the trees," Squish said.

"I didn't think they would," Magnus said. "They don't care about anything apart from their own business. So no meeting, then?"

"Oh no," Squish told him. "I'm going to have the meeting even if it's just me on my own."

EIGHT

IN WHICH A MEETING IS HELD

Squish felt very small as he went into the clearing in the middle of the woods. The sun had disappeared behind the trees and the tall trees cast very long shadows across the clearing. From the Woods, he could hear the birds twittering their last messages of the day to each other. Squish stood in the middle of the clearing and looked around. Apart from the distant birds and the whispering of the evening breeze in the trees, there was silence. Squish had never felt so lonely. He should have known the other animals were too busy to come. The whole thing was a waste of time. He was just about to leave, when he heard a rustling in the undergrowth.

"I thought you might need some company," Whitetip said. Squish had never been so glad to see anyone in his life. He wanted to say that he had hoped that Whitetip would come and that now he didn't care who else turned up.

"Your Dad will kill you," he said instead. "And me."

"Who's going to kill you?" Brian said, pushing his

way through a knot of tall grass.

"Brian! Thanks for coming," Squish said. "But I think it's only us."

"No it isn't," said another voice behind them, and Colin too emerged from the bracken. "My Dad doesn't know I've come either."

"Oh yes he does," Ray said as he came out from the shadows. "And now everyone else does, too."

Squish could make out the glow of four of five pairs of fox eyes, blinking in the shadows.

"Is this where the meeting is?" added yet another voice, and Earthface and three other older badgers pulled themselves out of a hole at the edge of the clearing. Squish had not even seen that there was a hole until a soil-covered badger's head popped out of it.

"Yes!" Squish cried. "Yes it is!"

With a flutter a group of small finches landed on a branch nearby, chattering to each other. Then a shadow crossed the clearing and the unmistakable yellow eyes of Professor Otus could be seen looking out from another tree.

"The books can wait," he said. "I wanted to see what young Squish has learned."

Squish looked around, his heart pounding. Suddenly the clearing was filling up. Hedgehogs uncurled, mice scurried up close so they could hear. Rabbits appeared, ears first, out of holes in the ground (but made sure they were on the other side of the clearing from the foxes). Then there was a rustle in one of the trees on the edge of the clearing and one after another, Squish's parents, his brothers and sisters, Whitetip's father (who didn't look at all pleased) and all the older squirrels lined up along the branches. All of a sudden, it was silent again. Squish stood in the middle of the clearing, surrounded by all the other animals, friends and strangers alike and had no idea what to do next.

"Squish," Magnus said, "everyone has come to hear what you have to say. Don't you think you'd better say it?"

Squish still did not know what to say, until he felt a paw on his back and Whitetip firmly pushed him forward.

"Hello, everyone. Thanks for coming," he said, in a voice which was little more than a squeak. Then he glanced at Whitetip, cleared his throat and began again. "You all know that the Greys are coming. I know you don't think it has anything to do with you."

"Squirrels!" one of the foxes muttered.

"Let the boy speak," Ray said clearly in a voice which threatened what might happen to anyone who didn't.

"But it does, you know," Squish carried on. "It affects all of us. We squirrels have a secret, you see."

Squish stared up at his father and the older squirrels. The older squirrels all whispered to each other, and then to Squish's father. He looked Squish directly in the eye and then nodded slowly. *Tell them.*

"We all need trees," Squish said. "We live in them, or make our homes out of them. We even make books out of them. Some of us eat things that grow on them. We all need the trees so we can live."

"Well of course we know that," Earthface said and the other badgers nodded in agreement.

"We all know that!" echoed a hedgehog who Squish thought was called Spike. Most hedgehogs seem to be called Spike. They do not have much imagination.

"Shh!" Whitetip said angrily. The hedgehog snuffled, but said no more.

"What has this got to do with your problem with the Greys?" Ray asked impatiently.

"Everyone thinks that we squirrels hide nuts and acorns and then can't remember where we hid them. But," Squish paused for breath, "we know."

"That's your secret?" Ray asked. "Is that all? I think we're wasting our time here when we could be hunting."

At the mention of the word "hunting" several rabbits disappeared back down their burrows.

"Let him finish, Ray," Squish's father said. "Please."

"We hide nuts and acorns and pinecones because trees grow out of them," Squish said loudly.

There was a long pause. Then there was a bark of laughter from the foxes and some of the birds tittered along with them.

"Be QUIET!" a loud voice shouted and the laughter stopped. Professor Otus spread his wings and soared down to stand next to Squish and Whitetip. "What the young squirrel says is true-hoo!"

"You knew?" Squish asked, astounded.

"I read a lot of books," Professor Otus said. "Didn't I always say reading is good for you? Now tell them what you need them to do."

"The Greys want to take all the nuts and all the acorns for themselves. If they take them all, no more trees will grow. What will we do then? Where will we live? What will we eat? This will affect all of us, not just the squirrels. I know how we can all work together and stop the Greys from ruining our Woods."

There was a chattering and a twittering, and growls and snuffles as the animals and birds all spoke to each other. Then Ray and Earthface and an older hedgehog called Spike Senior all padded across the clearing and stood with Squish, Whitetip and Professor Otus.

"Well then young squirrel," Ray said. "What exactly do you want us to do?"

IN WHICH A SMALL SQUIRREL HAS TO CROSS A BIG BLACK PATH

The birds were the first to do their bit. They flew from the Woods over the fields nearby twitting and tweeting to each other and to every other bird they met.

"What a pity about the squirrels of the Woods!"

"Who'd have thought there would be so few nuts this year?"

"Have you heard about the squirrels? Worst year ever for acorns!"

"Serves the silly squirrels right for forgetting where they put them!"

Soon the rumours started to come back to them.

"You're from the Woods, aren't you? Is it true what they're saying? The squirrels have no nuts at all this year?"

"I heard that they're so hungry they have to eat leaves!"

And so, as rumours do, they got worse and worse. A greenfinch landed on a branch next to Squish to bring him news.

"It's working even better than you thought, Squish," she chattered. "If you believe what you hear, the Reds might have to leave the Woods and find food somewhere else!"

"You're doing a wonderful job," Squish told her. "Thank you."

Greenfinches don't blush, but if they could, this one would have turned into a redfinch.

"This might be enough," she said. "You might not have to do the rest."

"I wish that was true," Squish said. "But I think the Greys might be too clever to believe everything they hear."

"I'd better go," the greenfinch said. "I've just thought of a good one about seeing squirrels packing up all their belongings!"

"Good luck!" Squish called, but the little bird had already flown off chatting excitedly to her friends.

Below the branch where Squish sat, there was a great deal of activity. If anyone saw, they would have thought the rumours were true and the Reds were packing up to leave. There were flashes of red fur as squirrels scampered backwards and forwards through the trees and bushes. If you were quick, you could see that they were not moving their belongings, but they were all holding as many nuts, acorns and pinecones as they could carry. You would also have seen that a young female squirrel with a white tip to her tail waved to Squish every time she ran past. Rabbits could be seen bounding past carrying nuts. Even a couple of hedgehogs shuffled by, rolling large pinecones with their snouts. Squish hopped down from his branch as Scamp ran past, carrying two large horse chestnuts.

"I hope you're right about this!" Scamp called. "I've never carried so much in my life!"

"I hope so too," Squish replied. "How are we doing?"

"We've cleared some hiding places completely," Scamp said, stopping for a break. "The rest still have enough nuts and stuff in them to look like we still use them."

"And you've put everything ...?"

"In the hole the badgers dug, yes. The deer have pulled some branches down to hide it. Everyone's doing their bit, Squish. Maybe the Greys won't see the hole. Maybe we won't have to do the next bit."

"I wish that was true," Squish said. "But the Greys know about hiding things. They will look everywhere."

"You're the boss," Scamp said with a smile. "You don't fancy giving us a hand for a bit, do you?"

So for a while Squish too ran here and there collecting pinecones and nuts and acorns and dropping them into the long low hole the badgers had dug. Several times he ran past Whitetip, who was usually running in the opposite direction. They smiled and waved to each other, but did not have time to talk. The deer stood by to lift the branches which were hiding the hole as the animals dropped their treasures into it. The deer then carefully replaced the branches.

The animals worked all morning, and soon the hole was full of nuts, acorns and pinecones. As Squish's father dropped his last acorn into the hole, all the animals stopped for a rest. Squish looked around. Everyone was watching him. It was obvious they expected him to say something. He spotted Whitetip standing at the back of the crowd and suddenly felt very proud.

"Thank you all," he said. "Everyone has worked so hard."

"Squish," his father said, "it was all your idea. But I think I should do the next bit. If it goes wrong, we will need clever young squirrels here to think of more ideas."

"No," Squish said. "I started this. It will only work if everyone helps."

"What about us?" a hedgehog asked. "We don't run as fast as some of you."

"If I'm right," Squish said, "you will not have to run."

"But what if you're wrong?" the hedgehog asked.

"If he's wrong," Ray the fox growled, as he slipped out from behind a bush, "it won't matter anyway. The rest of the foxes are still on guard around the Woods, by the way. Any sign of Greys, well, let's just say none of us had breakfast this morning. Why don't we just guard this hole?"

"We don't know how many Greys are coming," Squish said. "There might be too many for you to stop them all."

"Just as you say," Ray said. "We are prepared for whatever might happen."

"Thank you," Squish said. "Perhaps if the birds could spread the word that we are ready? We need everyone to come here, pick up everything they can carry and meet me at the place we agreed."

The birds did their job again, this time with whispered tweets in the ears of any animal they saw. Squirrels, rabbits, deer, badgers and foxes, even mice and voles all stopped what they were doing and quietly picked up nuts and acorns in their paws or their mouths. When they all arrived at the meeting place, Squish was waiting for them. Again, he could see that all the animals wanted him to say something. He hopped up onto a tree stump so everyone could see him.

"Thank you all," he said. "Animals have never worked together like this before. We only have one thing to do now. I know it is very dangerous and everyone will understand if anybody wants to stay behind. No-one will blame you."

There was silence for a moment, and nobody moved. Then the silence was shattered as one of the Nofurs met-all boxes roared past on the big black path right next to where they were all gathered.

"That's it! I'm going home!" Scritch shouted and all the animals laughed apart from some of the smaller ones who did not realise Scritch was joking.

"Are we all ready?" Squish asked. There was a chorus of squeaks, barks, tweets and snuffles.

Squish picked up his acorns, waited for a moment until he could not hear any met-all boxes rumbling toward him. He was suddenly aware that Whitetip was standing next to him. She held his paw tightly in hers.

"Squish," she said quietly. "Come on."

Squish held his breath and ran and ran.

And that is how Squish, with Whitetip at his side and followed by the biggest procession of all the different kinds of animals who lived in the Woods that anyone would ever see, came to cross the big black path.

TEN

IN WHICH WE FIND OUT
WHAT HAPPENED NEXT

You might remember that day. It was the day the Rangers in the Woods heard that lots of animals had gathered by the side of the road. They stood in the road and stopped all the cars while the animals all scampered, hopped, shuffled and ran across the road and disappeared into the bushes on the other side. The Rangers scratched their heads, hardly able to believe what they had just seen.

You may have seen photographs and videos of it on your favourite sites on the internet. If you look very closely at the pictures, you will see that all the animals were carrying nuts and acorns and pinecones. Squish was right, you see. When animals do funny things, we Nofurs like to stop and take pictures. Then, when something even funnier happens and everyone takes pictures of that instead, we all forget about the last one.

The animals, however, did not forget about that day. There were things which no-one but the animals knew. Only the animals knew about the tunnels the badgers had dug underneath the big black path so that no animals would have to cross it again to get home. They are big tunnels and took a long time to dig, otherwise Squish and his friends would not have had to cross the path in the first place.

And the Greys? Well, the Greys still have not arrived. Maybe the birds' rumours did the trick and they decided not to bother coming if there were no nuts to find. Maybe they heard that the Woods were being guarded by foxes who had not had any breakfast. Maybe they were never coming to the Woods at all. That is the trouble with rumours. You never know if they are true, so it is best not to listen to them.

When it became apparent that the Greys would not be coming after all, the animals worked together one more time to bring all the nuts and acorns and pinecones back to the Woods. This time, though, they used the tunnels the badgers had dug. After that, they all went back to doing what they do. Only the squirrels kept on thinking about the future and their childrens' futures.

And Squish? Squish carried on dreaming. I don't think anything could ever stop him. The older squirrels wanted to give him a new name in honour of his bravery, but he refused.

"I'm Squish," he said. "That's who I am."

"But you're unsquishable," Whitetip added, and everyone seemed to think that was just perfect. The older squirrels called him Squish The Unsquishable for a while. To his friends and family, though, he was always just Squish.

One day, not long after the nuts and acorns had been brought back, Squish was sitting with Whitetip on a low branch in the Pine Woods one morning. Since crossing the big black path together, Squish and Whitetip were rarely apart. Colin and Brian had not liked it much at first, but after a while they got used to it and treated Whitetip as one of their gang. Brian was snuffling around in the soil for something, and Colin was sitting alert and listening for noises in the bushes.

"Do you think the Greys will ever come?" Colin asked.

"I don't know," Squish replied. "But the trees are safe for the future. That is the most important thing. If they do come, though, I have another idea ..."

That idea will have to wait for another day because at that moment, Squish was interrupted by his mother's voice calling from the drey.

"Come on, Squish!" she called. "Stop daydreaming. Those nuts won't gather themselves!"

Squish and his friends will be back in the Spring after their hibernation...

... when Colin's adventure begins!

And finally ...

No book happens by itself and there are always lots of people to thank.

Bob: Thanks to Tony Higginson of Formby Books for constant support, encouragement and advice, and for 'Squish' in the first place; Alex Stone for typesetting genius in turning a book designed by a complete amateur into this professional publication, and last but by no means least to Wendy Stone for love, patience and wisdom always.

Holly: Thanks to my lovely Mum, Wendy for all of her support, advice and guidance on my illustrations. Her ideas and suggestions have a great eye for detail and are very much appreciated. Thank you to Tony Higginson for giving me the opportunity to display my art and for all his support. I'd also like to thank Mr. Collins and Mrs. Clark for being brilliant art teachers. Lastly I would like to acknowledge my Dad, Maurice (Boris), who although no longer with us, is still very much with us in spirit.

Squish would also like to mention the National Trust at Formby for their wonderful work in maintaining probably the most important red squirrel colony in the country.

39345827R00045

Made in the USA
Charleston, SC
08 March 2015